Magic Mirror

Orson Scott Card
Illustrated by Nathan Pinnock

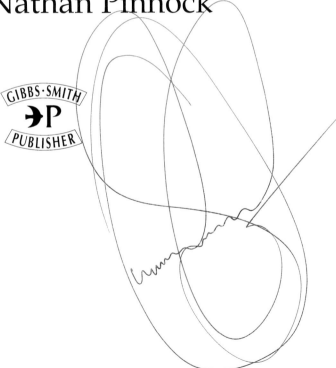

GIBBS·SMITH PUBLISHER

First Edition

03 02 01 00 99   5 4 3 2 1

Published by
Gibbs Smith, Publisher
P.O. Box 667
Layton, Utah 84041
Web site: www.gibbs-smith.com
Orson Scott Card's Web site: www.hatrack.com

Design by Nathan Pinnock

Printed and bound in China

Library of Congress Cataloging-in-Publication Data

Card, Orson Scott.
    Magic mirror / Orson Scott Card : illustrated by Nathan Pinnock. -- 1st ed.
       p.   cm.
    ISBN 0-87905-876-5
    I. Pinnock, Nathan.   II. Title.
PS3553.A655M34   1999
813'.54--dc21   99-27497
                                    CIP

Heather's life had been a beautiful dream. She grew up as a princess, always preparing herself to be a wise ruler of a great kingdom. She would be kind and generous, clever and resourceful, hand in hand with the man who was worthy to become a part of her life. One day she married a prince and began to live in the happily-ever-after that all her dreams had promised. Twenty years later, Queen Heather had become mistress of the palace, and her husband, Richard, was king, sallying forth every day to do battle with dragons and bring home treasures.

But time played some cruel tricks. King Richard hardly had time to speak to her now, leaving early and coming home late, when he came home at all. He did not seem to think he was part of her life. Instead, he seemed to think that she was a part of his—and not the most important part. Worse yet, at age fifteen their beautiful daughter, Alexandra, was apparently cursed by a passing witch, turning her ugly and ill-tempered. Queen Heather found that despite all her learning and all her trying, she was not particularly wise or clever, nor generous, nor resourceful. Some days she barely managed even to be kind.

All Queen Heather's hopes settled on their son, Jason, who was still bright and eager. So when Jason decided not to be a prince and went off to wizards' college, it almost broke her heart. King Richard noticed her unhappiness, and because he did want her to be happy, as long as it didn't take too much time away from his work, he obtained a magic mirror for Queen Heather, so she could see images of their son when she talked to him, no matter how far away he was. Queen Heather was happy for a while, until Jason got so busy at school that he never had time to converse with her, except to ask for gold.

HURRICANE ORSON

With her family no longer interested in her, Heather was barely interested in herself. Her own life, her own kingdom, were so empty that she began to command the magic mirror to show her a wider world.

She learned of tragedies and celebrations in faraway lands. She talked to strangers. After a while some of them became dear friends, who cared more about her than the people who ate at her table or slept in her bed.

Trash

As the days passed, she found herself talking more and more to one man, a minor wizard in a far-away country. He said she had a beautiful soul. He wrote her poetry. He cared about her. When she spoke to him, she felt young and beautiful again. His name was Stephen.

Queen Heather no longer cared about her own kingdom, for no one there seemed to care about her. She slept late, she ate little, and she never bothered about how she looked except when she thought that Stephen might see. Now it was Alexandra who fretted and Heather who refused to talk.

Alexandra journeyed to the battlefield where her father struggled endlessly with the dragons. He only had a moment to speak to her between onslaughts of the enemy.

"What is it, Princess?" King Richard asked her.

"Something's wrong with Mother," said Alexandra. She tried to explain.

"It sounds as if she's sad," King Richard replied. "We must cheer her up."

Then he plunged back into the fray, and Alexandra returned to the castle, more worried than ever, for now she knew her father could do nothing against the spell that had been cast on her mother.

One day the wizard Stephen was very sad. Heather asked him why, and he would not tell her. "I looked where I had no right to look," he said, "and saw what I had no right to see."

"Tell me," she insisted. "Let there be no secrets between us."

"It's not my secret," said Stephen.

"Whose secret is it?" asked Heather. But before he showed her the images he had found, she guessed the secret and it filled her with despair. It was King Richard's secret. It was King Richard's image.

Alexandra knew something was wrong even before she entered the castle.

Alexandra ran through the castle, fearing that some intruder had pierced the defenses. She called out for her mother, searched every room for her, not knowing whether to hope or dread that she might find her.

She found her mother weeping in grief.

There had been no intruder. The queen herself had ransacked the castle. But there was not a word of explanation from the queen, who wandered through the rooms as if she were a ghost.

Then, without warning, for no reason Alexandra could discern, Queen Heather ran from the room, mounted her steed, and fled the castle alone.

Alexandra was so worried that she prayed for God to watch over her mother and keep her from harm. In that moment, the spell of ugliness that had so long kept the princess captive was broken. All it had taken to restore her to her former beauty was to care with all her heart for someone else.

As she wandered through the castle, trying to think of what to do to help her mother, trying to imagine what it was that had caused the queen such grief, Alexandra could not help but glance at her face in each glass she passed—until she happened to look into her mother's magic mirror, and saw quite a different image there.

Alexandra dared not disturb the magic mirror, but she had to speak to her brother, Jason. She thought of the seashells given to King Richard by Naiads whom he had saved from a sea serpent who had tried to take over their small kingdom. Didn't Jason have one with him when he left for school? Could her father's shell be somewhere in the castle?

She found it by the sound of pounding surf that came from the shell, and shouted her brother's name above the roaring of the sea. Soon he had the other shell in his hand, and she told him all that she had seen.

Jason was not encouraging at first. "The only way to get inside the spell that governs her mirror is if I know her word of power."

"But all she ever says at the mirror is your name," said Alexandra.

"My name!" cried Jason. "Of course! Give me half an hour and I'll tell you what I discover."

"We might not have that long," said Alexandra. "I'm going to look for her."

Soon, astride her father's second-fastest mount, Alexandra was off in pursuit of her mother. But she had no skill at tracking, and if there was a trail she could not see it. All she could do was wander through the village and then out into the wild country where it was not safe for her to go.

When she saw her mother standing over the water, Alexandra knew her prayer was answered. She had come unthinkingly to the bridge that separated her father's kingdom from the barony where her mother had grown up. It was on this bridge that they plighted their troth some twenty years before.

"Mother!" cried the princess as she slid down from her steed. "For the sake of my love for you, take not another step!"

But Heather was under the spell of the mirror, and she saw only the road leading back to the dreams of her childhood, the hopes of her youth. She saw the life she thought she would earn by marrying the dashing prince who wooed her with flowers and poetry at her father's little castle in the countryside.

Somehow she had lost her way. But now she could have her dream again. The wizard Stephen had promised her. All she had to do was take a step and the road would carry her to the land of happily-ever-after.

A voice was calling to her, but it belonged to someone that had ceased to love her long ago. Heather raised her foot to take a step.

Alexandra pressed the seashell to her mother's ear, and above the crashing of the surf she heard the voice of her son, Jason, crying out to her.

"Mother! The mirror lied to you! I saw it in the lights and shadows! Father was never with this woman. I found the scenes that the wizard changed by adding that woman's face. It was you that father kissed so lovingly. It was to you he fed those tidbits at the table. All those years, there was never anyone but you."

The words cut through the fog in Heather's mind. As if awakening from a dream, she turned and saw not the ugly spellbound daughter of this morning, but the beautiful daughter who had loved her long ago, and heard the voice of her son like the sound of the sea.

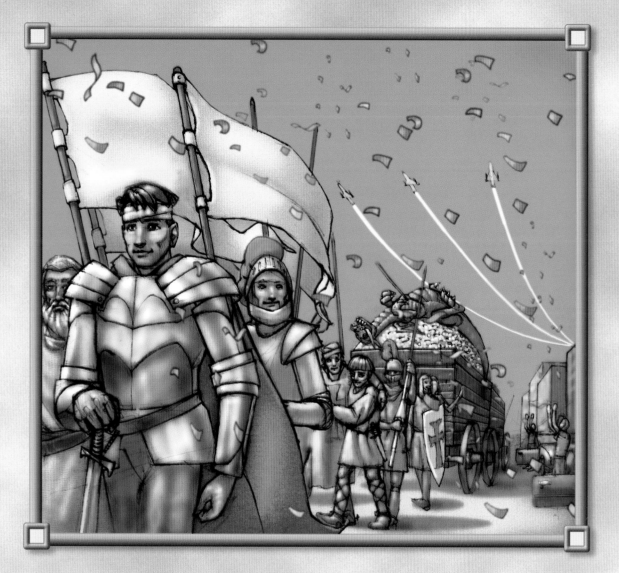

"I traced the spell," said Jason. "There was no wizard Stephen. A witch named Stephanie wanted vengeance on Father for a great defeat he inflicted on her kingdom. It was *her* face you saw in those twisted images. Father never loved her. She was his enemy."

At that moment, kind providence made Heather's relief and joy complete, for along the high road came King Richard, flush with victory.

"Ah, my beloved," said Richard, when he heard the tale, "our enemy could not have deceived you if I had not already broken your heart. Let the wars fight themselves. We have lands and gold enough for now. If you want me, I will be with you."

"And I with you," said Heather, "always with you, if you want me."

"All is well," said Alexandra into the seashell.

"Tell Father I did my share of hacking and piercing today," said Jason. "And tell them both I love them."

"I'll tell them," said Alexandra. "But they know."